Buzz off, Stephanie!

As soon as Stephanie and I stepped out the front door of the school, we saw Jenny Carlin and Angela Kemp sitting on one of the benches near the playground.

"She doesn't look nearly as perky as she did this morning, does she?" Stephanie said thoughtfully.

In fact, Jenny's mean little face was screwed up into a major scowl.

Then Stephanie actually called out, "Hey, Jenny — did you get it, or not? Are you Ms. X, the new advice columnist for our school paper?"

I couldn't believe it!

"Buzz off, Stephanie!" Jenny screeched. "You, too, Lauren Hunter!"

Look for these and other books
in the Sleepover Friends Series:

Stephanie's Big Story

Susan Saunders

AN
APPLE
PAPERBACK

SCHOLASTIC INC.
New York Toronto London Auckland Sydney

ISBN 0-590-42299-5

12 11 10 9 8 7 6 5 4 3 2   9/8 0 1 2 3 4/9

Printed in the U.S.A.   28

First Scholastic printing, August 1989

Chapter
1

"Okay, kids, we've seen that there are three kinds of stories in a newspaper," Mr. Whitney was saying. "News stories, which stick to the facts; feature stories, which give facts but also entertain the readers; and editorials, which give opinions."

Five B, our fifth grade class, was on a field trip to the offices of the *Riverhurst Clarion*. That was the first part of a project Mrs. Mead, our teacher, had dreamed up for us. The second part would be putting together our own weekly newspaper.

Mrs. Mead was nodding enthusiastically as Mr. Whitney talked — he's the owner of the *Clarion*. She was also keeping an eye on us to make sure we were all paying attention.

"You've met our police reporter, our sports reporter, some of our photographers . . . ," Mr. Whitney went on.

"You could be a photographer for the school newspaper, Kate," Stephanie Green whispered to Kate Beekman. Kate's been borrowing her dad's thirty-five millimeter camera lately, and she's taken some terrific pictures.

". . . our restaurant critic . . ."

"That's a natural for you, Lauren," Kate murmured to me — I'm Lauren Hunter, and I do love food. Doing reviews of restaurants would give me a fabulous excuse to eat out a lot!

". . . the society writer . . ."

"I'll take that one," Stephanie said to us in a low voice. "There's nothing I like better than parties."

"You've also seen how important the editors are, because they decide what to cover and whether or not the stories are fair, and they pull the reporters' writing together and correct mistakes," Mr. Whitney said.

"Patti," Kate and Stephanie and I all whispered at the same time. Wasn't Patti Jenkins the best at adding finishing touches to homework? She'd be a great editor.

Patti smiled shyly. She's one of the smartest kids in our class, and she's the fourth member of our gang.

"Now we're going downstairs to the basement, so that you can see this evening's edition of the *Clarion* actually being printed," said Mr. Whitney.

"Please stay together, class," Mrs. Mead called out as all twenty-six of us trooped through the newsroom and followed Mr. Whitney down the stairs.

"Wow — the floor is shaking!" Larry Jackson exclaimed. "It must be an earthquake!" He grabbed the banister and pretended to be hanging on for dear life. Pete Stone and Henry Larkin and some of the other guys were cracking up.

"Larry, that's enough!" Mrs. Mead warned.

"It's only the printing presses," Karla Stamos sniffed. She's always happy to show off what she knows. Karla used to be just plain boring, but this year she started taking this public speaking class after school, and she's gotten even harder to bear. I haven't liked her much since she insisted on telling me how to improve my grades a few months ago.

Ahead of us, Mr. Whitney pushed open the

heavy doors at the bottom of the stairs, and we could see the presses. They were enormous — about half a block long and two stories high — and the noise they made was unbelievable! Practically all the kids covered up their ears, except Henry Larkin, who played air guitar in time to the thump and bump.

Huge rolls of paper unwound through the machinery, where they were printed, folded, and cut apart into finished newspapers. Mr. Whitney gave each of us a fresh paper as a souvenir. Then he led us out a side door, shook hands with everybody, and told us we should seriously consider a career working at a newspaper. Finally we climbed into the school bus for the ride back to Riverhurst Elementary.

"Please look through your copies of the *Clarion*, class," Mrs. Mead instructed from her seat at the front of the bus. "You may come up with some ideas for our own newspaper."

Kate opened her *Clarion* and turned the pages slowly. "Like 'Around Our Town' could be changed to 'Around Our School,' " she suggested.

"Good, Kate," said Mrs. Mead.

"And 'People and Places' might work as 'Kids and Places,' " said Stephanie as we rolled around the corner of East Main Street onto Hillcrest.

" 'Club News' and 'Social Notes' would work just the way they are," said Patti.

"Rivvv-erhurst El-eeeee-mentary!" announced Mr. Dannon, the bus driver. "Watch your step!"

We had thirty minutes left before school was over for the week, and Mrs. Mead spent the time calling for volunteers.

On one side of the blackboard she wrote, "Reporters," and under that she wrote, "Around Our School, Sports, Club News, Social Notes, Upcoming Events." On the other side of the board, Mrs. Mead wrote, "Editors, Photographers, Artists."

"Don't forget," she said as she put down her chalk, "that reporters will automatically increase their written language grade."

Larry Jackson had been groaning about extra work, but he suddenly looked up and started waving his arm wildly. "Sports!" he practically shouted.

"He's thinking about that C minus he got on his last paper," Kate murmured to me.

And I was thinking about my C plus, which wasn't so great, either. It's not that I can't write. It's more what Mrs. Mead calls my presentation — my spelling's not wonderful, mostly because I forget to look things up or can't find my dictionary, and I have

5

trouble with commas from time to time. It doesn't help any that my papers, like my room at home, are pretty messy.

"Fine, Larry," said Mrs. Mead, writing his name next to "Sports" on the board. "Now, starting at the top, what about reporters for the school news in general?"

"Will the paper be about the whole school, or just our class?" Mark Freedman asked.

"The whole school!" Stephanie spoke up. "Otherwise, it'd be really boring — we already know what's going on with each other."

Mrs. Mead nodded. "That's a good point."

Nancy Hersh raised her hand. "I've got brothers in kindergarten, second, and sixth," she said, "and I'm in fifth, so I should be able to pick up some news from four grades at least."

Mark Freedman and Jane Sykes said they'd like to do school news, too.

"Three reporters should be able to handle 'Around Our School,'" said Mrs. Mead. "Next is 'Club News.' Karla" — she looked at Karla Stamos — "this might be something you would enjoy — " She didn't get any further, because Karla interrupted.

6

"I'd prefer to be in charge of 'Social Notes,' Mrs. Mead," Karla said quickly.

"Social Notes," by Karla Stamos? I couldn't believe my ears! First of all, who is *less* social than Karla? She's the biggest grind in fifth grade. Studying is fine — I mean, Patti studies hard — but Karla does nothing but study! When she's not *in* school, she's studying *for* school, or taking lessons to make herself a better student. I mean, she has absolutely no social life at all!

Secondly, she doesn't exactly have a lot of friends — especially since she started giving everybody unwanted advice about how to do their homework better, bragging about her own grades, and hogging class discussions. How could Karla write about parties when she hardly ever gets asked to any?

Thirdly, as I said, she's pretty dreary. I mean she practically lives in brown — her favorite color — which gives you some idea of her personality: dull, very, very dull.

Stephanie couldn't believe her ears, either. She sits in the first row of 5B, right in front of Kate and me, and her right arm almost shot out of its socket as soon as Karla opened her mouth.

"Mrs. Mead, Mrs. Mead!" Stephanie called out.

"What is it, Stephanie?" Mrs. Mead asked.

"I was really hoping to write 'Social Notes,' " Stephanie said. "I worked on the newspaper at my old school. . . ." She didn't bother to add she was only eight at the time.

"Well, with all the birthday parties and costume parties and dances and school get-togethers around here, I think there's plenty to keep two reporters busy, don't you?" Mrs. Mead said soothingly. She looked first at Karla, and then at Stephanie.

"Oh, yes, Mrs. Mead!" Karla replied brightly. On top of everything else, she's always buttering up the teacher.

"Yes, Mrs. Mead," Stephanie said glumly. She looked over her shoulder and rolled her eyes at Kate and me.

Kate raised her hand then. "What about a restaurant review," she suggested, "of places around town that serve the kinds of food kids like — telling whether or not the food's any good, how much it costs . . . that kind of thing."

"I think that's a wonderful idea!" said Mrs. Mead. "Shall I write your name down for it?"

"Oh, no — not me," Kate said. "It's perfect for Lauren."

Chapter
2

Kate's always putting in a good word for me —
we've been friends for years. Not that I can't rely
totally on Patti and Stephanie, too. But way before
there was either of them, there was Kate and me.

Kate and I both live on Pine Street, with only
one house between us. We were playing together
when we were still in diapers. By kindergarten, the
two of us were best friends.

That was about the time the sleepovers started,
too. Every Friday night, either Kate would sleep over
at my house, or I would sleep over at hers. The
Sleepover Twins, Kate's dad named us.

Not that we were ever anything like twins. Kate's
small and blonde; I'm tall and dark. She's one of the

neatest people around; I was *born* messy. Kate couldn't care less about sports; I'm kind of a jock. She's very sensible; I let my imagination run away with me from time to time. Still, I like to think I loosen Kate up a little, and I know she settles me down sometimes.

So we couldn't have been more different. But we couldn't have been closer friends, either. We never had a serious argument.

At least, not until Stephanie Green came along. That was last year, in fourth grade — Stephanie and I were both in 4A, Mr. Civello's class.

She and her family had moved from the city to the other end of Pine Street, and I loved hearing her stories about the things she'd done there and the famous people she'd seen.

Stephanie knew tons about the latest fashions. She already had a style of her own — she usually wears red, black, and white, which goes great with her black curly hair. And she was an excellent dancer. She also made me laugh a lot. I had a terrific time with Stephanie, and I wanted Kate to get to know her, too.

After that first sleepover with all three of us,

though, I knew it wasn't going to be easy. Kate made it clear she thought Stephanie was an airhead who was only interested in shopping. Stephanie thought Kate was a stuffy know-it-all. My older brother, Roger, said they couldn't get along because they were too much alike: both bossy.

But I didn't give up. Since we all live on Pine Street, we naturally started riding our bikes to school together. Then Stephanie invited Kate and me to her house for a sleepover. We gorged on Mrs. Green's yummy peanut-butter-chocolate-chip cookies and watched three movie classics in a row on Stephanie's own TV set. Kate's a real movie freak, so she had nothing to complain about *that* evening.

Then I asked Stephanie to my house again. Finally Kate gave in and asked her, too, and slowly the Sleepover Twins became a threesome. Stephanie and Kate didn't suddenly agree about everything, though. Not by a long shot. Which was one reason I was so glad when Patti Jenkins turned up in Mrs. Mead's class, along with the three of us.

Patti's from the city, too — she and Stephanie even went to the same school there for a couple of years. But you'd never know it to talk to her. Patti's as quiet and shy as Stephanie is outgoing. She's also kind and thoughtful, good at sports, and even taller than I am!

Stephanie wanted Patti to be part of our sleepover gang. And Kate and I both liked her right away — so it wasn't long before there were *four* Sleepover Friends.

We spend most of our free time together. Each one of us would stand up for the others, no matter what — I'd do practically anything for them, and I know they would for me. And there are no secrets between us. Usually.

"Lauren, would you be interested in trying the restaurant reviews for our paper?" Mrs. Mead was asking me.

Why not? It sounded like fun. And my overall written language grade could stand some improvement.

I nodded. "Yes, Mrs. Mead — I could work on my presentation. . . ."

"Her presentation might need work, but nobody can beat her at eating," Jenny Carlin said in a stage whisper to her sidekick, Angela Kemp. They both started giggling their heads off.

Jenny Carlin loves to get in her digs at me. Not

that she's wild about Kate or Patti or Stephanie, either. In fact, she doesn't have much time for girls at all. But she's really been on my case ever since Pete Stone started liking me instead of her at the beginning of the year.

Pete's changed his mind about a hundred times since then, and as far as I'm concerned it's history now. But Jenny's never forgiven me, even though I had nothing to do with it. She's so boy-crazy herself, she's convinced that I planned the whole thing.

"I have an idea," Jenny screeched while Mrs. Mead was writing my name on the board. Jenny has a shrill, scratchy voice that sets your teeth on edge.

"Yeah — Jenny wants to write a column called, 'Boys, and How to Trap Them,' " Kate said just loud enough for Jenny to hear.

Jenny made a face in our direction, but it didn't slow her mouth down. "How about an advice column," she said to Mrs. Mead, "like 'Ask Sylvia' in the Sunday *Clarion*?"

I hated to admit it, but Jenny had actually said something interesting.

"An advice column?" said Mrs. Mead. "That's a clever idea."

"We could have a box in the hall for questions — I'd be glad to answer them," Jenny said, totally smug.

"See . . . I wasn't so far off base," Kate murmured to me. " 'If you want a boy to notice you look at him out of the corner of your eye and flutter your lashes. . . ,' " she added, pretending she was Jenny, giving advice.

"It's important for the writer of an advice column to be able to say exactly what she, or he, thinks," Mrs. Mead was saying. "And that's not easy if everyone knows who the writer is." She considered for a second. "I'll tell you what we'll do — anyone who is interested in writing an advice column, including Jenny, of course, should come up with a question and a suitable answer by Monday morning. I'll read them all and choose the best, and that person will be our advice columnist. No one will know who he or she is except me and the editor in chief of the newspaper. Fair enough?"

Everyone agreed that it was fair, but Jenny looked kind of pouty. I guess she'd pictured herself the star of the show, with half the school hanging on her every word.

Mrs. Mead took a few more volunteers for reporters. Then she asked for photographers, and Kate volunteered herself, along with her dad's camera. Sally Mason signed up to be an artist — she's the best doodler in school. We decided on the editors last. Just before the bell rang, Patti was elected editor in chief of our paper by the whole class.

"Think of a name for the newspaper over the weekend!" Mrs. Mead said as we scraped back our chairs, grabbed up our homework, and stuffed our books into backpacks.

Kate, Patti, Stephanie, and I headed down the hall and out the front door of the building together.

"Step on it! I have a horrible feeling Karla's hot on my trail!" Stephanie said as she hurried us toward the bike rack.

We'd pulled our bikes out and were just about to pedal up Hillcrest when Nancy Hersh yelled, "Hey, Stephanie — wait a second!"

She trotted over to us to say, "There's a sixth-grade party tomorrow afternoon that you might want to check out for 'Social Notes.' My brother Andy's going." Andy Hersh is Nancy's older brother, the sixth-grader.

"Who's having it?" Stephanie asked her.

"Leslie Macklin — it's her twelfth birthday," Nancy said.

"I know Leslie, sort of," Stephanie said. "I see her at the Health Club on Main sometimes." The Greens have a family membership — Stephanie's not big on exercise, but she does go swimming once in a while. "Do you think I should call her and ask if she wants it written up in my column?"

"Why not?" Kate said. "Leslie's nice — her dad works at the hospital with mine." Kate's father's a doctor.

"It sounds like a good party — about forty kids, and her parents even hired a deejay!" Nancy said.

"Whose party?" It was Karla Stamos, horning in on the conversation! "Is it something we could cover for the *Fifth-Grade Flyer*?" she went on. "I just thought of that name — isn't it great?"

"It sounds like a sled," Kate mumbled to me.

I could almost hear Stephanie groaning to herself. "Oh, nobody's," she said out loud, answering Karla's first question. When Karla raised her eyebrows in disbelief, Stephanie added, "Only a sixth-grade party that a fifth-grader would never get asked to anyway."

Just then a beige station wagon pulled up at the curb and beeped its horn. "Where there's a will

16

there's a way, co-reporter," Karla said. "There's my mom. Toodles."

"Toodles?" Kate said as the Stamoses drove away. "Ick! Where does she get these expressions?"

"It must be the same place she gets her clothes," Stephanie said, climbing onto her bike. "A store that carries everything boring. And *I'm* stuck with her!"

"You are *such* a snob," Patti said softly.

"Well," Stephanie said, "maybe I am, but I'll probably *never* change."

Kate smiled and nodded her head.

Chapter
3

The sleepover was at Stephanie's house that Friday. Actually, it was at Stephanie's playhouse. At least, that's what anyone else would probably call it. Stephanie calls it her apartment — she says it sounds more sophisticated.

What does a kid who has practically everything — her own phone, her own TV, her own VCR, her own fifteen-speed — get for her eleventh birthday? Her own apartment, natch!

Okay, it's basically just one big room, and it's in the backyard of her parents' house, and she can only spend the night there when she has all of us to keep her company — in fact, this was going to be our first sleepover at the apartment.

But it's really neat, with cute little windows and a skylight, a small fridge in the corner for munchies, enough room for the four of us to sleep comfortably, a tiny bathroom, and . . . no adults!

"The rug came!" Stephanie said excitedly as she led Kate and Patti and me through the backyard that evening. "Wait till you see it!" She unlocked the door and turned on the light.

"It's great-looking!" I said. The rug was a red-and-black tweed that went perfectly with the two gray-and-white fold-out couches.

"And the curtains are up!" Patti said.

They looked terrific, too — mostly red, but with tiny black and white squiggles.

"Couches, curtains, rug — is there anything you still have to get?" Kate asked her.

"Oh, a table for the TV, maybe a chair, some stuff on the walls. . . ."

"What about a phone?" I said, half joking. Phones are important at sleepovers — you never know when you might have to dial a request into WBRM–Riverhurst, or who might have to call somebody up in the middle of a game of Truth or Dare. Still, I didn't really expect even Stephanie's parents to install a new phone line to the apartment.

19

"We've got a phone," Stephanie said. She reached for the receiver, which was lying on the counter next to the refrigerator. "It's Dads, but we can use it whenever we're out here. It's a cordless."

"How does it work?" I'd seen cordless phones in stores, but I'd never used one.

"Right now the base is plugged in in my bedroom," Stephanie said. "When somebody calls my number, it beams the signals over here. . . ."

"As long as the receiver is within a thousand feet of the rest of the phone," Patti added, "it will pick up the signals. My mom has one in her office."

In fact, the receiver rang while we were talking about it. Stephanie switched it on. "Hello?" she said. ". . . Oh, hi, Leslie. Your mom told you I called? . . . Right — I'm going to be doing 'Social Notes' for our class newspaper. . . . No, it's not just for fifth grade — it'll have articles in it about everything that's going on at school. . . . Uh-huh. And I heard you're having a party tomorrow, so I wondered if . . . Karla Stamos? When? . . . I will — we're both writing the column. . . . Okay. Forty-two Jagger Lane at three tomorrow afternoon. . . . Great — see you then."

Stephanie switched the phone off. "How did

Karla even hear about it? Nobody talks to her!" she exclaimed. "Can you believe that sneak, calling Leslie behind my back?!"

Kate giggled. "But, Stephanie," she said, "you were going behind Karla's back."

"Wouldn't you? Can you imagine having to show up at any party with her, let alone a *sixth-grade* party?" Stephanie said glumly. "Totally gruesome!"

"I don't think I'd be willing to go to Leslie Macklin's party alone, especially if I were Karla," Patti said. "Maybe you should call her and find out if she's serious about it."

"Yeah — if I'm lucky, she'll have to take one of her weekend classes instead," Stephanie said, brightening a little. "Besides, I feel like telling her off! All that baloney about 'co-reporter,' when she was trying to scoop me!" Stephanie got the Stamoses' number from information. She punched it in and waited. "Hello? . . . Oh, hello, Karla," Stephanie said, wrinkling her nose at us. "I just spoke to Leslie Macklin. . . . Really?" Stephanie covered the mouthpiece of the phone and whispered, "She was *just* going to call me, right?" . . . "Umm-hmm," Stephanie said to Karla. "Forty-two Jagger Lane, at three. . . . Fine. . . . I guess I'll bike over." Stephanie paused. Then, "Where do you live, Karla?" she asked. "Nineteen Maplewood Drive. . . . Listen, since your house is on the way from mine to Leslie's, why don't I stop by, and we can ride over together. . . . Great. I'll see you around two-thirty. Bye." After Stephanie hung up, she added, "That girl has got to stop saying 'toodles.'"

"First you complain about having to hang around with Karla. Then she tries to scoop you. And now you're making plans to spend even more time with her than you have to," said Kate. "What gives?"

"Get to know your competition," Stephanie answered. "And if I have to show up at the party with her tomorrow, I'm going to make sure Karla looks as good as she can look," she added.

"Good luck!" I said.

"Check this out," Stephanie said, changing the subject. "Ta-da!" She flung open the door of the little refrigerator. It was stocked with what looked like a lifetime supply of Dr Peppers, a big bowl of my special onion-soup-olives-sour-cream-bacon-bits dip, and a platter of Mrs. Green's peanut-butter-chocolate-chip cookies.

In the cabinet above the fridge were two king-size bags of nacho-cheese-flavored corn chips plus all the napkins, cups, and plates we could possibly need.

"This should get us through the next few hours, at least," I said, tearing open the chips.

"Which restaurants are you going to review this week, Lauren?" Stephanie asked, getting out four glasses.

"You think I have to do more than one?" I said around a mouthful of corn chips.

"Check with the editor in chief," Kate advised, pointing to Patti.

"It would probably be a good idea," said Patti, opening a Dr Pepper. "Otherwise, your column would be so short it would get lost. I'd aim for two or three restaurants a week."

"Okay, I'll do three. But I'll have to do them all tomorrow," I said.

Mrs. Mead wanted the first issue of our paper out by next Thursday, which meant all the articles had to be in by Wednesday morning. I couldn't eat out on Sunday, because my whole family was driving to Dannerville to watch Roger run in a marathon.

And I couldn't eat out on Monday or Tuesday because my mom's working now, and I have chores to do when I get home from school.

Could my stomach take three meals before dinner? Why not? I have a healthy appetite, and Patti had said our class fund would pay back the costs. I aimed some more chips at the dip bowl.

"I'll report on the Pizza Palace, the Burger Joint . . . and that new place, China Wall," I said. All three of them are at the mall, so I wouldn't have to waste time getting from one place to another. "But I hate to eat alone, guys. Kate, why don't you and Patti come with me?"

"I wanted Kate to go to Leslie's with me, and take some party pictures!" Stephanie complained.

Kate shook her head. "Sorry — I can't do either one. I promised my mom I'd help her paint the dining room tomorrow."

"What about you, Patti?" I said. "We could start with lunch at the Pizza Palace and go on from there."

"Okay — I'll check with Mom and Dad," Patti said.

"It'll take you a while to eat three meals, won't it?" Stephanie said. "I should be through at Leslie's by a quarter to four. Want to meet at Just Juniors at four?'' Just Juniors is at the mall, too. It's a great store for kids' clothes. "We can try on stuff — it'll give me something to look forward to, after Karla."

"Terrific?" I said.

Patti nodded. "I need some new jeans."

"I should be finished by then, too," Kate said.

"Great!" said Stephanie. "Four o'clock at Just Juniors. Now — let's check out *Video Trax*."

Chapter
4

Stephanie turned the TV on, we gathered up the food and the Dr Pepper, and spread out on the new tweed rug.

"It's Tangles," Stephanie said, looking at the TV set. Tangles is a British all-girl rock band with hair practically down to their knees. "Don't you think their lead singer looks like Jenny? Same button nose, same hair cut, same mean little eyes. . . ."

"Stop! You're ruining my appetite!" Kate said.

"What are we going to do about her?" I said.

"What do you mean?" Patti asked.

"The advice column! We can't just let Jenny have it!" I said.

"What have you got in mind?" said Stephanie.

"I have plenty to do, working on 'Social Notes.' Patti's editor in chief, you're busy with your restaurants, Lauren, and Kate'll be taking pictures."

"Maybe you could try for it, Kate," I said. "You won't be photographing every second."

"I think advice columns are dumb," Kate said. "I never read them. I don't think I could even dream up a question."

"Sure you could," I said. "You know, like, Just because I got a *D* on a math test, my mom grounded me for two weeks. Don't you think that's overdoing it? I mean, who needs math anyway — that's why they invented calculators. Signed, Twentieth-Century Student."

"Exactly. Or, Every time I say a boy is cute, I find my friend Amy batting her eyelashes at him three seconds later," said Stephanie. She demonstrated, looking just like Jenny Carlin. "Do you think a true friend would act like that? Signed, Bewildered."

"Maybe there are some questions in last month's *Teen Topics*," Patti said, picking up the copy that was lying on the nearest couch.

"No way," said Kate. "I'm going to stick to taking photographs and working on a project for the video club." Kate's very serious about being a movie director some day — she's already made a couple of short videos of her own.

"Well, that's that, I guess," Stephanie said. "Jenny's probably going to end up writing the advice column after all. Boy, she'll be great. She knows just how to offer helpful comments. Remember what she said about your hair that time, Lauren? 'I'm glad Lauren's finally started to take an interest in her looks.' In front of everyone in school. Ick!"

"Don't get me started," I said.

"Anyone with half a brain could do the column," Kate said suddenly. "It doesn't even have to be a girl."

"What about Henry Larkin?" Patti suggested. She sits next to Henry in 5B.

We thought about it for a split-second. Then we all started giggling.

Henry's smart enough, all right, but the idea of him asking for extra work is a joke. He's always getting into trouble for goofing off during regular school hours. And on top of being kind of lazy, he's just about the most laid-back kid in Riverhurst.

"Yeah, can't you see it?" Stephanie said. "Question: Dear Mr. Advice, my science report is due in two days, and I haven't even thought of a topic yet.

What should I do? Signed, Totally Panicked. Answer: Dear Totally, Tell your teacher you did the report, but your cat threw up on it." Henry actually used that excuse last year. "And chill out, man. Worrying is bad for your health. Signed, Mr. Advice."

"Did he even volunteer for anything this afternoon?" Kate asked.

"Yeah — artist, I think," Stephanie replied.

"Henry can't draw," I said.

"Ri-i-i-ight!" said Stephanie.

We were cracking up when suddenly there was a super-loud buzzing sound — all of us jumped.

"What's that?" Patti asked anxiously. "The smoke alarm?"

Kate started sniffing the air.

"No — the cordless." Stephanie scrambled to her feet to pick it up. "Hello? . . . Hi, Dad — we're fine. . . . Absolutely. If we need you, we'll buzz. . . . Okay. Good night."

"It's an intercom, too," Stephanie explained when she sat back down on the floor. "Dad can buzz us, and I can buzz the house. He was just checking to make sure we weren't getting nervous, out here by ourselves."

"Not yet," said Kate with a grin. "But if we catch

some of the *Friday Chillers*, who knows?'' She switched the TV to channel 21, which plays at least two scary movies every Friday night.

Kate nudged Stephanie, and they grinned at Patti and me. Nothing scares the two of them, but Patti's imagination is as spooky as mine is. Then Stephanie turned off the overhead light, and we settled in to watch *Strike Force from Cygnus X*.

Fortunately, it was pretty easy to take, because it was clear right from the start who the aliens were. They all had auburn hair and huge black eyes with no white around them, and they walked stiff-legged.

They talked by beaming thought waves back and forth to each other. The waves sounded like high-pitched bleeps — the kind computer games make. When the aliens got angry, all the bleeps would run together into one irritated shriek, and you knew that somebody was about to get fried.

I don't know how long it took for me to realize that some of the weird noises I was hearing didn't have anything to do with the movie. At first, I put them down to my runaway imagination — after all, I did once convince myself that Kate had really jinxed Patti. Then I thought maybe I was dozing off and dreaming the sounds, so I tried pinching myself.

30

But finally, after an especially long and piercing *beep*, I murmured, "Does anybody hear that besides me?"

"I-I do," Patti stammered.

"Uh-oh," Stephanie said. "Kate, do you think there's a rerun of *Farmer Brown's Neighborhood* on right now? Guaranteed safe enough for Lauren and Patti." As you've probably guessed, *Farmer Brown's Neighborhood* is a show for four-year-olds.

"Very funny," I said. "But I'm serious — I hear weird bleeping sounds, and they seem to be coming from somewhere inside this room. Turn the TV off."

"Just a second, Lauren," Kate said crossly. "We're right at the point where the aliens get wiped out by plain water. I've seen this before, and it's got incredible special effects: the Cygnians melt and turn into this bubbly green slime. . . ."

I reached out and switched off the TV.

The apartment was dead quiet for a second. Then we all heard it: three sort of chirpy beeps, followed by two deeper ones.

"So, am I crazy?" I said. "Or what?"

"What is that?" Kate said to Stephanie. "Is your dad trying to call us again?"

"I don't think so," Stephanie said. "The intercom is definitely more of a buzz than a beep." She stood up and looked slowly around the room.

"There it goes again," Patti said after a short, sharp beep.

"It *is* the phone," Stephanie said, edging over to it cautiously. "Maybe it has a loose wire or something. . . ." She picked it up carefully and switched it on. She held it to her ear. Then she frowned.

"Are you getting a dial tone?" Kate asked.

Stephanie put her finger to her lips in a silent "ssssh." Slowly, she walked over to us, still listening. Then she held the cordless out, so Kate and Patti and I could hear the faint voices, too.

"I'm *not* over-reacting!" a guy's voice exclaimed. "Were you talking to Craig Dyson, or not?!"

Craig Dyson's a senior at Riverhurst High, and he's pretty cute, too.

"Yes, I *was.* So what?!" a girl's voice replied angrily. "I've known Craig since second grade — why shouldn't I talk to him if I feel like it?"

"Who?" Kate whispered.

Stephanie shook her head for quiet, and all four of us leaned closer to the cordless.

"Because we're supposed to be going steady, remember?" said the guy. "You have my football jacket, my basketball sweater, my senior ring. . . ."

"They're history, even as we speak!" said the girl. "If you drive by my house, you'll see them — they'll be lying on the front lawn, right where I've thrown them!"

"Aw, come on, Mary Beth . . . ," the guy said.

Kate and Stephanie and Patti and I all nodded our heads — the mystery was solved.

Mary Beth Young is a junior in high school who happens to be Todd Schwartz's girlfriend. And Todd Schwartz — the quarterback of the Riverhurst High team — just happens to live across the street from the Greens.

Todd and Mary Beth are always breaking up, which is what we were hearing. But *why* were we hearing it?

"And what about you, Todd Schwartz!" Mary Beth's yell came through the cordless. "Weren't you walking down the hall with Shannon Brewster just yesterday — "

Kate took the phone from Stephanie. As soon as she'd switched it off, the weird beeps started again. "The cordless must make these sounds when it's picking up stray signals," Kate said.

"Right," Patti agreed. "It has a range of a thousand feet, so sometimes it'll pick up signals from anybody with a cordless phone who's living within a fifth of a mile of your house," Patti said. "The Schwartzes across the street, the Morisons next door, the Williamses behind. . . ."

"And probably police cars driving through the neighborhood, CB radios . . . ," Kate added.

Stephanie took the phone back and switched it on again — Todd and Mary Beth were still arguing. Stephanie turned it off. "Too bad," she said. "If we were printing high-school social notes, I'd definitely have a scoop here, Schwartz and Young Battle It Out."

"It wouldn't be much of a scoop," Kate pointed out. "They break up at least twice a month."

"Hey — I wonder how far apart Karla and Leslie Macklin's houses are," I said.

"You mean Karla could have heard about the party on a cordless?! I bet that's it, that . . . that . . . spy!" Stephanie said. "I'll find out when I'm over there tomorrow, and if she has one . . . two can play that game!"

We ended up watching *Strike Force* through to the end, when the green slime that used to be aliens bubbled into the sewers to grow stronger, and then part of *Twilight of the Vampires*. I ate everything in the apartment, the way I always do during scary movies. That's probably why I dreamed what I did: that the cordless phone beeped, I picked it up, and I heard Todd Schwartz admitting to Mary Beth Young that he was an alien from Cygnus X!

Chapter 5

"That's undoubtedly the reason Todd looks the way he does," Stephanie snickered when I told her and Kate and Patti about the dream the next morning. "You know — that pumped-up body, no neck; the little, round, bowling-ball-type head."

"Obviously the result of the low gravity on the planet Cygnus," Patti added in her most scientific tone.

All of us giggled. We were sitting in the Greens' big kitchen, scarfing down Mr. Green's special banana waffles with crispy bacon and real maple syrup, while Mrs. Green helped him — she's going to have a baby soon.

"Don't you think you ought to go easy on those,

Lauren?" Kate asked as I considered having seconds of everything. "You have about five meals to get through before dinner."

"Okay — just one more waffle," I said, pouring on the syrup. "If I start to feel too full, I can always run around the parking lot at the mall."

You know that old saying about not wishing for something too hard, because you just might get it? Well, nothing could have sounded better to me than being a restaurant reviewer. I'd get to eat a lot of my favorite foods, for free. I'd only have to write a couple of short paragraphs about each place, and Mrs. Mead would automatically raise my written language grade. Talk about having your cake and eating it, too!

By that night, though, I never wanted to see another French fry or egg roll, much less a piece of cake!

Everything started out fine.

Patti showed up at one o'clock, right on time. We strolled into the Pizza Palace, sat down at the counter, and ordered a small double-cheese pizza with pepperoni, meatballs, and olives, plus two king-sized Cokes. While John, the cook, put the pie together and slid it into the oven, I started to take notes.

"My mom showed me some restaurant reviews in her magazines," I told Patti. "*Setting* is one of the things they always talk about — how the restaurant looks."

I glanced around the Pizza Palace, which is just about the farthest thing from a palace you can imagine. It's a small room with the counter running along one wall, the pizza oven in the back, and four video games lined up on either side of the front door. At the moment two little boys were going crazy playing "Alien Attackers."

"Setting," I wrote in my notebook. "Small, clean, warm." As a matter of fact, the oven warms the place up to about a hundred degrees. "Entertainment center near door."

Then there was "service" to consider, which means how good the waiters are. There aren't any waiters in the Pizza Palace, but John is fast, and he never gets your order wrong.

"Service is very good, don't you think?" I asked Patti.

"Very," she said.

"Kind of food: Italian," I wrote. "Dress?" I said out loud.

Patti looked down at her sweats and sneakers,

at my faded jeans, and over at John's big blue apron splattered here and there with tomato sauce. "Definitely casual," Patti said.

As I was adding the prices to my notes, John slid our pizza out of the oven and cut it up. He served each of us a slice on paper plates, and left the rest of the pie on the counter between us.

"I'll finish this one up with a few sentences about what I ate," I said to Patti.

Since her mouth was full, she just nodded.

"Crust is tender and chewy, the cheese bubbly and rich-tasting, the meatballs and pepperoni spicy, but not too spicy. All in all, the pizza at the Pizza Palace is excellent, the service very good, the prices reasonable. Highly recommended."

Then I closed my notebook, jammed it into my canvas tote along with my pen, and got down to some serious eating.

By the time we were through at the Palace, my three slices of pizza, not to mention the extra banana waffle, were sitting a little heavily in my stomach.

When we got outside, I touched my toes twenty or thirty times, and ran in place for a couple of minutes. I don't recommend it as a cure for eating too much. Afterwards I felt even worse! But duty is duty.

I took a deep breath and threw back my shoulders. "All right," I said to Patti. "On to the Burger Joint!"

The Burger Joint looks pretty much the way you'd expect from its name. There's a grill in front near the window, and a bunch of wooden booths crammed into every inch of the rest of the space.

Patti and I sat down in a booth near the grill and checked out the menus the waiter handed us.

"A tunafish sandwich," Patti said. "And a glass of iced tea." She was starting to fade already, I could tell, because her usual at the BJ is a hot turkey sandwich with fries and a Coke float.

"A deluxe cheeseburger," I told the waiter bravely. "A side order of onion rings, and a vanilla milk shake."

Okay, that might have been overdoing it. But I was a restaurant reviewer, wasn't I? I had to have something to review.

I think I would have been all right if Larry Jackson and Henry Larkin and Mark Freedman hadn't wandered in about that time. They were carrying baseball gloves and bats — an afternoon of practice was probably Larry's idea of sports reporting.

"Hey, boys," our waiter said as they plopped down in the booth next to ours.

"Hey, Jim," Larry said, grinning at us. "Taking good care of our restaurant writer?"

Patti and I started shaking our heads and frowning at the guys. I mean, you're not supposed to *tell* the restaurant that you're reviewing it. You want them to treat you like a regular customer.

But Jim the waiter was already asking, "What do you mean, 'restaurant writer'?" He stared down at Patti and me.

"Lauren." Henry nodded at me. "We're starting a school newspaper, and Lauren's reporting on Riverhurst restaurants that kids might like."

"Everybody at Riverhurst Elementary'll be reading it," Mark said.

"Ah." Jim nodded thoughtfully.

He strolled over to the grill, and I saw him talking to the cook. A couple of minutes later, he came back carrying a tray with the food Patti and I had ordered on it.

Jim set the tunafish sandwich and the iced tea down in front of Patti. He served me the cheeseburger, onion rings, and shake.

41

But he didn't stop there: he added a green salad with Thousand Island dressing, a big bowl of vegetable soup with noodles, and a huge piece of German chocolate cake.

"I didn't order all this!" I said. There was at least fifteen dollars worth of food crowded onto my side of the table.

"Compliments of the chef," Jim said with a little bow.

The cook waved at me and smiled.

I shook my head. "I can't keep this food — it wouldn't be right."

"If you send it back, the chef's feelings will be hurt," Jim said, looking sad.

"So will my stomach's," said Larry. He scooped up a spoonful of German chocolate cake.

"Relax, Lauren," Henry said. He reached over to grab an onion ring.

I glanced at Patti, who shrugged her shoulders. What could I do? I really felt as though I had to eat all of the food, so I wouldn't offend the chef. And the guys weren't much help. They wouldn't touch the green salad and the vegetable soup, and they left me with a third of the cake.

Even though the cook tried to argue, I insisted

on paying for the meal at least. Patti and I said good-bye to the guys and headed out into the mall again.

"China Wall's at the other end of the main aisle," Patti said to me. "Ready to roll?"

"Roll is about all I can do," I groaned. "I feel as though I've swallowed a beach ball." Waffles, pizza, hamburger, soup, salad, cake. . . . I didn't want to think about it. But we were off to the China Wall.

It's a neat-looking place, with one of those keyhole-shaped doors, a little fountain near the cash register, and real tablecloths.

Fortunately, there were no other kids from Riverhurst there, which made me feel better. At least nobody was going to tell any of the waiters that I was a restaurant reviewer. On the other hand, our waiter did take a deep, personal interest in how much we enjoyed our meal. He kept encouraging me to eat and I *couldn't* let him down.

I ate every single bite of an egg roll and an order of sweet-and-sour pork — plus the rice it came with — and then I staggered back through the keyhole-shaped door. I made it as far as the nearest bench in the main aisle and collapsed in a heap. "There's more endurance involved in being a restaurant writer than in being a runner," I said. I jog three times a week with my brother, Roger.

Patti checked her watch. "Uh-oh — it's almost time to meet Kate and Stephanie at Just Juniors."

"It's all the way back in the other direction!" I moaned. "But I guess I'll be needing a whole new wardrobe — at least two sizes larger — if this keeps up. Lead the way."

"We'd better hurry," Patti said, dashing up the aisle.

"No way," I said, waddling after her. "You go ahead — I'll get there eventually."

When I finally caught up with Patti, she was talking to Stephanie outside the store. I could see right away that Stephanie had had some problems of her own that afternoon. She was wearing her black-and-white checked pants, her red hightops, her black leather jacket with red trim . . . and a brown sweater?!

"What happened to you?" Stephanie asked as I trudged slowly toward them. "Your face is absolutely green."

"You seem to be changing colors yourself," I said, pointing at her brown sweater.

"In a word: *Karla*," Stephanie said grimly. "I wanted to glitz her up a little for Leslie's party, but she didn't have a single thing in her closet worth wearing. So I lent her my red sweatshirt."

"Did she look better than usual?" Patti asked.

"No," Stephanie said, "but *I* definitely looked *worse* than usual. And I felt that way, too, after five minutes at the party. It was so embarrassing watching Karla stalking around, taking notes in that stupid notebook. She even interviewed the deejay."

"Oh, no," I said.

"And then she started following me every-where," Stephanie went on. "Every time I got in a conversation, I'd notice that the person I was talking to was looking off to my side. I'd turn that way, and there she'd be, writing down everything we were saying!"

"Stephanie, that's awful," Patti said sympa-thetically.

"Even that wasn't as bad as when she actually asked Mrs. Macklin how much the party cost her per guest — right when I was taking a bite of cake. This *has* to have been the worst afternoon of my life. It's almost enough to make me want to give up 'Social Notes.' You don't think Karla planned it that way, do you?" she added suspiciously.

"I don't think she's that crafty," I said.

"*She* may not be, but there's someone who is."
Kate had arrived just in time to follow Stephanie's
stare. Jenny Carlin and Angela Kemp were waltzing
out the door of Just Juniors, absolutely dripping with
shopping bags.

"Stephanie!" Jenny exclaimed, flashing a phony
smile as she checked out the brown sweater. "Did
you suddenly go color-blind? Or are you trying to
look more like your co-reporter?"

"Listen here, Carlin . . . ," Stephanie began, her
cheeks flushing a bright pink, the way they do when
she's boiling.

But Jenny had turned to me. "We have to run.
We're meeting Steven Gitten . . . and *Pete*, of course
. . . at the movies. And don't forget — if any of you
need help with boys, just drop a note in the box in
the hall. I'll be happy to answer it in the paper!"

"Pete Stone must have dough for brains!"
Stephanie muttered.

"She's really incredible," I said as Jenny and
Angela walked off.

"She'll get hers someday," Kate said.

Chapter
6

"Let's get inside, quick!" Stephanie said. "I have to do something about this sweater, before anybody else sees me!"

"Just aim me at the Husky sizes," I said, heaving myself through the door of Just Juniors. "I keep thinking about this python I saw on TV once. It swallowed a zebra, and then it didn't eat again for a whole week. Do you think that's how it's going to be with me? Stuff myself at three restaurants every Saturday for the review, and then digest for seven days?"

"Gross me out, Lauren!" Stephanie said. "What about this?" She reached into a stack of sweatshirts and pulled out one with thick red and black stripes.

She held it up and studied herself in the full-length mirror.

"It's a great look," said the saleswoman, Michelle. "Mixing patterns is this season's fashion statement, and stripes go with *everything.*"

"I'll take it," Stephanie said to Michelle. "I'll charge it to my mom's account, okay? My mom lets me do that. I'll wear it home." She stepped into the dressing room to put it on.

Patti found some jeans to try on, and I picked up a pair with suspenders. "My stomach can't take a belt right now," I said. We followed Kate into the dressing room.

"Did Karla have a cordless phone, Stephanie?" Kate asked as she slipped into a cool-looking embroidered denim jacket.

"I didn't see one." Stephanie threw the brown sweater on a chair and pulled the red-and-black sweatshirt over her head with a sigh of relief. She shook out her curls. "Karla could have hidden it, of course. Anyway, it doesn't matter — I've got the jump on her now."

"Oh, yeah?" I said, adjusting my suspenders. "How?"

"I heard it from Andy Hersh, while Karla was bothering people with interviews. He told me that there's going to be a surprise party for Mimi Harris after school on Tuesday at Ekhart's Rink. Since Karla doesn't know Mimi or any of her friends I don't know how she will ever hear about it."

"Unless she's riding up and down the streets of Riverhurst with her cordless, picking up stray signals," Kate teased. "Do you think my mom would let me pay for this out of my allowance, Lauren?"

I looked at the price tag. "Sure — for a hundred and ten dollars, that should take you well into next year."

"Did you and your mom get your painting done?" Patti asked as Kate took the jacket off with a sigh.

"Painting? Oh . . . uh . . . yeah. We were mostly touching up the corner of the dining room that peels. Which reminds me" — Kate looked at the neon clock over the door of the dressing room — "I've got to get home by five-fifteen. My dad's fixing dinner."

Dr. Beekman is a fabulous cook, but for once I wasn't even curious about what he was making.

"I'd better go, too," Patti said. "We're having

company from Mom and Dad's department tonight."
Both of Patti's parents are history professors at the
University.

"I'm ready," Stephanie said, stuffing the brown
sweater into the shopping bag Michelle gave her.

Patti and I changed back into our own sweats
and jeans, and the four of us biked home.

That Sunday, I could barely choke down half a
grapefruit for breakfast, and I passed up the ham-
salad sandwiches Mom had packed for us to eat in
Dannerville. It wasn't until the middle of the afternoon that I could manage anything — and even then
it was just a banana from the picnic basket. I really
wasn't looking forward to the steak dinner I knew
Mom was planning. Was my reviewing career ruining my eating career?

When I rode my bike to the corner of Pine Street
and Hillcrest on Monday morning, Kate and Patti
were already there, gabbing away. They stopped
when they saw me. Kate stuffed some papers into
her backpack.

"Am I interrupting something?" I said.

"Just talking about the newspaper," Kate said.

"Hi, guys," said Stephanie as she braked to a

stop beside us. "Today's the big day."

"What big day?" Kate asked.

"The day Mrs. Mead decides whether or not Jenny Carlin gets to be impossible in print for the next few weeks. When do you think she'll make up her mind, Patti?"

"She'll probably read the questions and answers during lunch," Patti said.

"Then I'll keep my left fingers crossed until one o'clock," Stephanie said, showing us. "Anybody would be better than Jenny — I'd rather have Karla Stamos!"

"Let's not go overboard," Kate said.

We pedaled down Hillcrest toward Riverhurst Elementary.

"Don't I see something brown standing near the bike rack?" I said to Stephanie.

"Oh, no! Karla, first thing Monday morning, is too much!" Stephanie groaned.

But they greeted each other with great big smiles.

"Any hot news?" Stephanie said, sounding as friendly as can be.

"Nothing yet," Karla answered sweetly.

"Oh — before I forget — let me return your

sweater," Stephanie said, digging it out of her backpack and handing it to Karla in a crumpled ball. "Thanks for lending it to me."

"I really enjoyed borrowing your sweatshirt, too," said Karla. She pulled Stephanie's red sweatshirt out of her brown canvas tote. It was a mass of wrinkles.

"I don't think I can stand another second of this," Kate murmured to me. "They're going to kill each other with politeness."

Stephanie and Karla just stood there with frozen grins for a second. Then Stephanie asked, "About Leslie's party — I think we should combine our notes, don't you? Hand them in as one big article from both of us."

Karla shook her head. "Noooo . . . I think we should keep our notes separate. That way, the editor in chief" — she smirked at Patti — "can decide what's worth keeping and what should be *thrown out*. There's the bell. Toodles."

"I'm going to strangle that girl!" Stephanie growled as Karla made a beeline for the door. "She thinks her writing is *much* too good to get mixed up with my crummy scribbles!"

"Forget Karla — we're going to be late," said

Kate, steering Stephanie up the sidewalk.

After the second bell had rung and we were sitting at our desks, Mrs. Mead said, "I'd like the questions and answers from all of you who are trying out for the advice column. And just to be certain that the identity of the winner stays a secret, I want everyone in class to fold a piece of paper in half — only *you* will know if your paper is blank or not — and pass it to the front of the room."

"Nuts!" I whispered to Kate as we opened our notebooks. "I thought if only three or four people handed in questions and answers to Mrs. Mead, we'd be able to figure out who won."

Twenty-five pieces of white notebook paper, folded in half, were passed up to Mrs. Mead's desk. The twenty-sixth piece was pale pink, with hearts around the edge.

"Leave it to Jenny," Stephanie murmured over her shoulder.

I glanced over at Jenny Carlin, who had a self-satisfied smile on her face.

"She's so sure she's going to win!" I whispered back.

Then Stephanie wriggled her crossed fingers behind her back.

"By this afternoon, we'll know if Stephanie's charm works," I said to Kate.

"How are we going to know that?" Kate said. "It's a secret."

"Patti will tell *us*," I replied confidently. Don't we tell each other everything?

"Does anyone have suggestions for what to call the advice column?" Mrs. Mead was asking.

"Everything You Ever Wanted to Know . . . ," said Mark Freedman.

". . . And Then Some," added Pete Stone.

"Thank you, boys, but that title is a little long," Mrs. Mead said.

"Words of Wisdom," Karla offered, to the sounds of gagging from Henry Larkin and Larry Jackson.

"Tips from Terry," said Donny McElroy.

"Who's Terry?" Steven Gitten asked.

"I don't know — it just goes together." Donny is such a dork!

"How about Q&A, by X?" Jane Sykes suggested.

"Way to go!" said Henry Larkin. "It sounds like a rock group — U2, or UB40."

"I like it, too, Jane. It's simple and to the point," Mrs. Mead said. "Class?"

Everybody agreed, except Karla, who shrugged her shoulders and sniffed.

Then we threw around some names for the paper. They were all pretty much the same — stuff like the Sentinel, or the Journal, or the Courier. So it blew everybody away when Patti raised her hand to say, "How about It's Elementary?"

"Very nice, Patti!" said Mrs. Mead. "For those of you who haven't read any Sherlock Holmes detective stories, 'Elementary' was one of his favorite expressions, meaning 'it couldn't be more basic.' If we used the name for our paper, the 'Elementary' could refer to Riverhurst Elementary, and it could also say that we're covering all the basics of school news."

"I think it sounds excellent!" Kate said.

"It'll look great on the front page," Sally Mason added, and she does have an artist's eye.

"All in favor?" Mrs. Mead asked.

"Aye!" It's Elementary had won by a landslide. Our paper had a name.

Chapter
7

Patti wasn't nearly so helpful about coming up with the name of Ms. or Mr. X of Q&A, though. Stephanie and I pounced on her as soon as school was out for the day.

"I was watching to see who Mrs. Mead talked to this afternoon," I said. "But she talked to practically *everybody!*"

"So who is it?" said Stephanie.

"Mrs. Mead really meant it when she said she didn't want anyone to know," Patti told us seriously. "Listen — I have to get downstairs right away. Ms. Gilberto" — she's the elementary school art teacher — "is going to show Sally Mason and me how our press works."

"Can't you just say if it's Jenny Carlin or not?" Stephanie asked her, just as Kate appeared.

Patti shuffled her feet and looked very unhappy.

"No, she *can't*," Kate said firmly. "Patti has a job to do, and *we* have jobs to do. And right now, I have to photograph the sixth-grade play practice in the auditorium. Want to come?" she asked Stephanie and me.

"Sure — I told Mom I'd be a little late getting home, anyway," I said. I'm supposed to call her at the office as soon as I get to our house. "I need to pick up some typewriter paper for my article."

Stephanie answered, "Why not? Maybe I'll beat Karla to some party news."

"Sorry, Patti," I said before we left. "I didn't mean to put you on the spot."

"Yeah — I'm sorry, too," Stephanie said. "We'll find out in four weeks, anyway, when *It's Elementary* goes out of business."

"Right," Kate put in.

Patti cleared her throat. "Thanks, guys — see you tomorrow."

Kate collected her dad's camera from the principal's office — she'd left it there for safekeeping — and we walked down the hall to the auditorium. At the door we ran straight into Karla Stamos, on her way out, clutching her notebook.

"Hi, Stephanie. I've already covered play practice," Karla said briskly. "There's no need for you to go over the same ground." Then she marched off down the hall.

"*Gah!*" Stephanie flopped down onto a folding chair with her hand to her forehead. "She's like a nightmare, the kind you have over and over again! And since when is play practice 'Social Notes'?"

"Yeah, it's really 'Around the School,' " Kate said. "Mark Freedman and Jane Sykes had better watch out."

"I might as well go home," Stephanie said, disgusted.

"I guess I will, too," I said. "I want to start typing up my reviews."

We left Kate taking a picture of Ricky Delman, one of the leads in the sixth-grade play. As soon as Stephanie and I stepped out the front door of the school, we saw Jenny Carlin and Angela Kemp sitting on one of the benches near the playground.

"She doesn't look nearly as perky as she did this morning, does she?" Stephanie said thoughtfully.

In fact, Jenny's mean little face was screwed up into a major scowl.

"I really want to know, don't you?" Stephanie said to me.

"Sure, but . . . ," I was beginning, when Stephanie actually called out, "Hey, Jenny — did you get it, or not? Are you Ms. X?"

I couldn't believe it!

"Buzz off, Stephanie!" Jenny screeched. "You, too, Lauren Hunter!"

"Temper, temper," Stephanie murmured. "Well, that makes me feel a lot better — at least Jenny's doing worse than I am. Now that we're sure it's not her," Stephanie went on, "maybe I'll write Ms. or Mr. X for advice about Karla."

"You're kidding!" I said.

"Karla will read it, along with everybody else. Maybe she'll recognize herself and back off," Stephanie said as we unlocked our bikes for the ride to the stationery store. "Don't say anything to Kate, though, okay? You know what she thinks of advice columns."

"Okay," I said. "If you don't want me to."

"Definitely not," Stephanie said firmly. 'I don't

need Kate *and* Karla on my back." Then she changed the subject. "What about stopping for ice cream at Charlie's after we get your typing paper?"

The idea made me so queasy I thought I'd have to stop my bike. I hadn't made it through a whole meal since Saturday. "Uh . . . I don't think so, Stephanie," I said as soon as I could manage it. "I really have to get home and start . . . dinner."

I spent that evening using Roger's typewriter to get my reviews into shape. Something in me — like my stomach — really wanted to get them out of my sight so that I could have room to think about whether I should continue in this reviewing business. I mean, I didn't much like the fact that writing about my favorite foods was making it impossible to eat them. Anyway, I actually turned the reviews in to Mrs. Mead the next morning, a day *before* the deadline.

"My goodness, Lauren — what a pleasant surprise!" Mrs. Mead said. "This is early, it looks well-organized, it's certainly neat" — me, neat, can you believe it? — "and I can see your written language grade improving by leaps and bounds. Patti will take a look at this tonight, and we'll get it on the word processor tomorrow. Good work!"

Of course, after that, I felt a little better about the whole thing. Maybe I could try being restaurant reviewer for one more week. At any rate, I was off duty until Saturday.

Stephanie was still having problems, though. When she showed up at the party at the skating rink that afternoon, she found Karla had beat her to the punch again.

"There she was on skates, with her dumb note-book, glomming onto Matthew Yates, Andy Hersh, Taylor Sprouse" — Taylor, who thinks he's the coolest guy at school! — "asking them totally embarrassing questions, like, 'What's your favorite color?' " Stephanie said on the phone that evening. "And where did she hear about the party? I'm beginning to think Karla has ESP!"

"Did you write to X?" I asked.

"Yep — I dropped it in the box in the hall when I went for a drink of water this afternoon. I can't wait for Karla to see it — she'll know right away who it's about," Stephanie said. "Well, gotta go write up my column."

Wednesday morning was the deadline for everybody's articles. Patti and the other editors, Robin and Erin and David, went over them, correcting grammar and spelling and making sure they made sense.

After lunch, one of the kids on the paper typed up all the pieces on the word processor. And that afternoon after school, Kate and Stephanie and I and some of the other kids helped Patti, editor in chief, get *It's Elementary* ready to print.

Ms. Gilberto showed us how to cut out the typed articles, glue them down properly, and add headlines and photographs — Kate's of the play rehearsal were really funny, especially one of Ricky Delman standing on his head. But I didn't see the page with my restaurant reviews on it, or the Q&A column.

Neither did Stephanie. "Nancy Hersh and I were working on the 'Around Our School' page. I didn't get a look at 'Social Notes,' " Stephanie said after Kate had turned into her own driveway that evening. The two of us were pedaling farther down Pine. "Not much longer, though — we'll see it tomorrow afternoon."

Mr. Hathaway, the custodian, delivered three hundred copies of *It's Elementary* to 5B at about three o'clock on Thursday. Mrs. Mead held the top one up in front of the class.

"Our own newspaper — quite an accomplishment!'' she exclaimed, and everybody clapped. ''We'll distribute the copies outside the front door as the students leave for the day. Henry'' — Mrs. Mead handed a stack of papers to Henry Larkin — ''and Sally'' — she gave some to Sally Mason, too — ''and Larry will help me carry the rest. There's the bell. Let's go, group.''

So Kate and Patti and Stephanie and I got our copies on our way out. We ran over to a bench near the playground, sat down, and started reading.

''Wow! My reviews look great!'' I said. Maybe I *would* stick with it the whole month, I thought. Then I started to giggle. ''Who did the drawing?'' At the top of my column, under ''Kid Food,'' there was a sketch of me sitting behind a table piled with burgers and onion rings and cake, with a totally sick expression on my face. ''It's perfect!''

''Henry Larkin,'' Patti answered. ''Can you believe it?''

''He's really good,'' said Kate. ''Who would have ever imagined?''

''Patti,'' I said after a minute, ''don't you think that with the art and all, and maybe a little more detail next time, the column would be big enough if I just reviewed *one* restaurant a week?''

Patti laughed. "I think so, Lauren. Let's ask Mrs. Mead tomorrow."

Stephanie was scanning 'Social Notes' on page three. "There's still a lot of my stuff in here!" she said. "It's not all Karla's. Thanks, Patti."

"Your writing is a lot more fun than hers is, Stephanie," Patti pointed out.

"Wow — I knew there was something I forgot to tell you," Kate said suddenly. "It's about Karla."

"What about her?" Stephanie asked.

"How she finds out about parties," Kate said. "Her aunt and uncle own The Party Store on West Main Street! I went there with my mom for some wrapping paper yesterday, and I noticed their names on the door: 'Victor and Ethel Stamos, Owners'! And mom told me that Victor and Karla's dad are brothers!"

"So every time somebody comes into the store to buy paper, or cards, or party decorations, they hear about it!" I said.

"Right. And they tell Karla," said Kate.

"So it wasn't ESP or cordless phones! No wonder Karla wanted to do 'Social Notes' — she knew she'd look like an ace!" Stephanie said. Then she glanced down at the paper again. "Where is Q&A?" she asked casually.

"Um . . . on the back page," Patti said.

Stephanie and I both flipped to page six and started to read. There was a question about whether or not you should tell if you see a friend doing something against the rules. There was one about what to do if somebody likes you and you don't like him.

"These are excellent," I said when I got to the end of the second one.

"Yeah," Stephanie said, " 'X' is pretty smart."

Then we both saw Stephanie's question:

Dear X:

I am working on a project with someone who is driving me crazy! She thinks she is a better reporter, a better writer, even a better dresser than I am. She is so pushy and bossy I don't think I can take much more. Do you have any suggestions on how I should handle her?

Disgusted

And the answer:

Dear Disgusted:

You say your co-reporter is pushy and bossy — I say she's trying to be helpful. Don't be so quick to criticize. Instead of looking for faults, you should be taking full advantage of her talents. Learn all you can from her writing, her reporting, maybe even her dressing. It sounds to me as though she has a lot to offer, and you're lucky to have her.

X

Oh, no! I groaned to myself.

"What kind of clown is responsible for this column?!" Stephanie screeched when she'd finished reading a couple of seconds later.

"What's that supposed to mean?" said Kate. "You just said '*X*' was smart!"

"*I* sent this question in," Stephanie said, thumping the paper, "because I wanted Karla to know how I felt. Now Ms. or Mr. X, the X-pert, is telling me I should *learn* from her?! Patti — " she added with a dangerous glint in her eye.

"*You* wrote the question?" Kate interrupted. "But I thought *Karla* had written it about *you!* The stuff about being a better dresser. . . ."

66

"*You* thought!" Stephanie stared at Kate, and Kate stared back. "Are you saying that you're X?"

Kate didn't answer, but she did do something she hardly ever does — she started to blush.

"Thanks a lot, friend!" Stephanie said grimly. "And thanks for telling me, Patti."

"I couldn't . . . ," Patti began.

But Stephanie was off and running. "And double thanks to you, Lauren — I'm sure you knew all along, because Kate never keeps any secrets from you!"

"I didn't . . . ," I started to say.

That's when Stephanie threw her copy of *It's Elementary* down on the ground and stamped away, her cheeks a bright red.

Chapter
8

"Yeah, thanks a lot for always telling me everything, Kate!" I said. "Patti had a job to do, but what's your excuse?" I jumped up off the bench, too, but Kate grabbed the back of my sweater and pulled me down again.

"I only did it because one of us had to at least *try* to beat out Jenny Carlin," Kate said. "Patti had to know, because she was going to see it anyway, but I was too embarrassed to tell you and Stephanie about it. You know what I think about advice columns. And then when I actually won!"

"Yeah, well — that's exactly why Stephanie didn't want me to tell you about her question," I said. " 'Don't say anything to Kate — you know what she thinks of advice columns.' ''

"You knew she was writing in?'' Kate squawked.

"If you'd told us the truth, she never would have done it. Besides, why didn't you recognize her hand-writing?'' I said. Stephanie's handwriting is big and round, like a whole series of *O's*. You could pick it out of a stack of homework papers in about three seconds flat.

"The question was *typed*,'' Kate said. "When I read the stuff about 'better dresser,' and . . . and 'pushy and bossy,' I figured it had to be Karla writing about Stephanie. And if you look at it that way, my answer was pretty nice.''

Stephanie had jerked her bike out of the rack on the other side of the front sidewalk. Without even glancing in our direction, she shot up Hillcrest so fast it was hard to believe she didn't leave a streak of black tire rubber on the pavement!

"Now what do we do?'' Patti said.

"Let's go over to my house and call her,'' I said.

But when we got to my house and dialed Stephanie's private number, we let it ring twenty times and didn't get an answer.

"I'm sure she's there,'' Kate said, hanging up at last.

"Why don't we try Mrs. Green?" Patti said.

"Good idea," said Kate.

Mrs. Green picked up her phone right away, but we didn't get much farther. "No, I'm afraid Stephanie isn't taking any calls just now," she said.

"What if we came over there, Mrs. Green?" Kate suggested. "Then we could explain this whole mis-understanding. . . ."

"It's not really the best time," Mrs. Green said. "Stephanie is quite upset. Why don't you let her sleep on it? I'm sure she'll feel better in the morning."

But the next morning Stephanie didn't show up at the corner of Pine and Hillcrest on her bike. Kate and Patti and I waited for ten minutes, until Kate looked at her watch and said, "If we don't leave right now we're going to be spending lunch hour with Mrs. Wainwright." If you're late more than once, you have to sit in the principal's office during lunch-time. It's an experience we've all had, and don't care to repeat.

We were racing down Hillcrest, halfway to school, when Mrs. Green's red car drove past us. Stephanie was in the front seat with her mom, and she stared straight ahead as we waved.

By the time we'd locked up our bikes and dashed into the building, Stephanie was already at her desk. She didn't glance up when we stumbled through the door. The final bell was ringing, and I tripped over Patti's feet, and we almost fell down. Henry and Larry and some of the other guys got hysterical, but Stephanie just sat there, looking miserable.

She didn't whisper a single comment over her shoulder to Kate and me all that morning, either. Not even when Jenny practically drooled on Pete Stone when they went to the board together during math class.

"This is very serious," I murmured to Kate.

At lunch, Stephanie sat with Erin Wilson and Robin Becker. She wouldn't even talk to Patti, who went over to try pleading our case. And she was out the door like a rocket when the last bell rang that day. When we got outside, all we saw was the back of the red car, making its way up Hillcrest.

"I guess that means she's not coming to my house tonight," I said. I was having the sleepover that Friday. "What are we going to do?"

Kate shook her head. "I got us into this mess. I'll have to think of a way to get us out."

* * *

Patti showed up at my house before Kate did that night. When I opened the front door she had on her backpack, as usual, but in her hand she was carrying the receiver of a cordless phone.

"What's that for?" I asked her as we climbed the stairs to my bedroom. "And where's the rest of it?"

Patti shrugged. "I don't know — Kate called me all excited a while ago and told me to bring just this part of my mom's phone."

Then the doorbell rang again, and Kate was there herself to explain. "I thought of a way to get all of us face to face tomorrow morning," she said proudly.

"How, when Stephanie won't even look at us, much less speak to us?" I asked.

"Do you think she still cares about 'Social Notes'?" Kate said.

"I don't think she'd quit and leave it to Karla," Patti said, "especially not after that Q&A."

"I agree with you," Kate said. "So I came up with this idea. The cordless phone inspired me."

Patti and I nodded, waiting.

"These things have a range of a thousand feet, right? And Emily Morison" — a sixth grader — "lives right next door to the Greens, probably not

72

more than a hundred and fifty feet away."

"Umm-hmm." What was Kate getting at?

"What if we pretended to be Emily Morison talking to . . . oh . . . I don't know — let's say Sara Wallace, about a party tomorrow? A party Stephanie might want to cover for 'Social Notes'?" Kate said.

I thought I was beginning to see. . . .

"But how would we work it?" Patti asked. "She won't answer her phone. . . ."

"She will if we hit this intercom button a few times" — Kate tapped the button a couple of times, and we heard Todd Schwartz-type bleeps instead of Mr. Green's *buzz*. "Stephanie will think she's picking up stray signals. She won't be able to resist. She'll grab the phone, she'll overhear party news, and she'll show up at Charlie's Soda Fountain tomorrow at eleven o'clock!"

Patti smiled. "It's possible. But Kate, we're a lot farther away from the Greens' than a thousand feet."

"That's the one small problem," said Kate. "We'll have to sneak down there later with the cordless and hide in the bushes."

"What?!" I said. "No way!" I mean, we've sneaked out at night playing Truth or Dare, but we've never gone farther than my house, or Kate's, or the

Fosters' in between us. "If my parents caught us creeping down Pine Street in the dark, I'd be grounded for the rest of my life!"

"I thought of that, too," Kate said smugly. "Roger's in training for the track team, isn't he?"

"Yes," I replied. "What does that have to do with anything?"

"He has to be home by eleven," Kate said triumphantly. "So we'll get him to drive us to Stephanie's then!"

"Are we talking about the same Roger?" I said. "Why would he agree to that?"

"I'll manage Roger. I'll *beg*. Let's practice the party conversation," Kate said. "You be Emily, Lauren, because your voice is kind of high, like hers is. Patti can be Sara Wallace, and I'll be in charge of bleeps and beeps."

We ran through it a bunch of times, even though I thought it was a real waste. Roger is not that helpful when it comes to Sleepover Friends' business.

But Kate waylaid him on his way in through the back door at ten-forty, and after a couple of minutes of whispered begging and pleading, he actually nodded his head. "You've got exactly thirteen minutes," he warned. "If Coach Barnard sees me out after eleven, I'm definitely dead meat."

Thank goodness Mom and Dad had gone to bed early. I raced upstairs for Patti's cordless, and the three of us piled into the back seat of Roger's old car.

"Thanks a lot, Roger. See, Stephanie wrote in to the questions and answers column of *It's Elementary* . . . ," Kate began to explain as we drove down Pine.

Roger held up his hand. "No details," he said, pulling over to the curb near the Schwartzes' driveway. "Just be back here in eight minutes."

We opened the car door as quietly as we could and streaked across the street. Then we pushed into the clump of azalea bushes between the Morisons' house and the Greens'.

"Not many lights on," I whispered, peering through the branches.

"Stephanie's probably watching TV — *Friday Chillers* has two zombie movies on," Kate murmured. "Okay — let's do it!"

She punched the intercom button on the cordless once . . . twice. Then she switched the phone on and held it out toward Patti and me.

"Hello, Sara?" I said. "This is Emily."

"Emily Morison?" Patti repeated, in case Stephanie had missed what I'd said.

Kate punched the button twice more.

"That's right," I said. "My cousin is here from upstate. You know her, Sara — Julie Morison?"

"Your cousin Julie is here?" Patti repeated.

A bleep from Kate.

"Ummm-hmmm. I'm having a little party for her tomorrow at eleven, at Charlie's Soda Fountain, and I'd like you to come," I said.

"A party for Julie at Charlie's Soda Fountain at eleven?" Patti said. We were beginning to sound like a broken record. "I'd love to come. Thanks, Emily."

Another of Kate's bleeps.

"See you, then," I said. "I wonder if we'll get written up in the paper? Bye."

Kate clicked off the phone. "Good job!" she whispered. "Let's get out of here!"

We were crawling back out of the azaleas when we heard some very heavy breathing not three feet away.

"What is that?!" Patti squeaked.

"*Bob!*" I groaned.

Bob is a half Dalmation-half Bassett who belongs to the Williamses, who live in the house behind the Greens. He's not dangerous, but he has the loudest bark in Riverhurst.

"Quiet, Bob — no need to get excited," Kate whispered soothingly. "You know us. . . ."

The engine of Roger's car suddenly coughed a few times across the street. "We'd better hurry — he might just leave without us," I warned.

We scrambled the rest of the way out of the azaleas, and Bob really started up. Just to make sure we'd gotten the point, he followed us across the street, still barking his foolish black-and-white head off!

Kate and Patti and I dove into the car, and Roger made a speedy getaway. But a lot of lights had flashed on at the Greens', along with most of the other houses around them.

"Think anybody saw us?" Patti said anxiously.

Kate shrugged. "We did our best."

We got to Charlie's Soda Fountain at ten-forty-five the next morning, just to be on the safe side. Charlie's is a neat old place on Main Street, with real antique stained-glass windows, a black marble counter, and wooden booths with such tall backs you can't see who's sitting in them.

Kate and Patti and I sat in the last booth, the way the four of us always do. At about five minutes to eleven, we ordered: a Coke float with two scoops of vanilla ice cream for Kate, a lime freeze for Patti — their usuals — a plain DP for the new me (I had my one review to do later, thanks to Mrs. Mead) . . . and a chocolate shake for Stephanie.

"What if she doesn't come?" Patti worried.

But Kate nudged us with her foot. We peered around the side of our booth in time to see Stephanie pushing open the revolving door.

Chapter
9

"Stephanie's here," Kate murmured to Patti and me. "But she might leave as soon as she sees us."

Stephanie didn't leave, though. She walked straight across Charlie's and slid into our booth as if nothing had happened.

"Hello, Emily, Sara, and Cousin Julie," she said with a completely straight face.

"You spotted us last night," I said.

Stephanie nodded. "With Bob after you like a huge, crazed black-and-white caterpillar." The corners of her mouth turned up. "I figured if you guys had gone to so much trouble. . . ."

"Listen — I'm sorry about your letter," Kate put

in quickly. "I'm resigning from that dumb column as of right now."

"You can't!" Patti exclaimed.

"Why not?" said Kate.

Patti shook her head and sighed. "Because the job will go to the person who came in second!"

"Who was that?" Stephanie asked, taking a sip of her chocolate shake.

"As editor in chief, I can't really say who," Patti began, ". . . but I *can* say that she sent in her entry on pale pink paper. . . ."

"Oh, no!" Stephanie and Kate and I shrieked.

"No way you can quit!" Stephanie said to Kate. "Besides" — she hesitated a moment — "I have to admit, I thought your first two answers were good." Then she cleared her throat. "Actually, the answer to my letter was good, too, and I can see how you thought Karla had written it. But by then I was so mad about her using her aunt and uncle as spies to make herself look like a star reporter. . . ."

Patti and I both grinned. Kate and Stephanie don't apologize every day, especially not to each other.

"How can I compete with that?" Stephanie went on. "I'm the one who's quitting."

"You can't!" Kate said. "With Karla writing them alone, 'Social Notes' will put everyone to sleep!"

"She scoops me right and left!" Stephanie threw up her hands. "Why fight a losing battle?"

"You won't have to — I've got an idea . . . ," I said slowly.

"What?" Kate, Stephanie, and Patti all turned to me.

"We *make up* a party," I answered, "then we feed it to Karla's aunt and uncle at the store, and teach her a lesson!"

"Let's do it!" said Kate, taking a last sip of her Coke float.

"Excellent!" said Stephanie. She finished her chocolate shake in one long gulp.

Patti pushed her lime freeze out of the way and scrambled to her feet.

"Hang on — does anybody have a pen?" I said.

"Sure." Patti handed me a felt-tip from her jacket pocket, and I started scribbling on my paper napkin.

"An invitation to the fake party?" Kate said, raising an eyebrow.

"No, a review of Charlie's," I said. "You and

Stephanie aren't the only reporters around here, you know."

The four of us rehearsed our story while we pedaled over to West Main Street. By the time we'd locked our bikes up in front of the Party Store, we had it down perfectly.

"Ready?" Kate said.

"Ready," Stephanie, Patti, and I nodded.

Kate pushed open the door and we marched inside.

The Party Store is small, and every inch of it is crammed with cards, ribbons, rolls of wrapping paper, and party favors. The only free space is behind the cash register, which is where one of the Stamoses always sits. That morning, it was Mrs. Stamos.

Mr. Stamos was arranging a display of birthday candles on one of the shelves. "Can I help you?" he said to us.

"No, thank you," Stephanie answered. "We're just looking at cards for a swimming party at the Health Club this afternoon."

"Here's a nice one," Kate said, holding up a card with kittens on the front. She raised her voice,

"Do you think *Heather Fordman* will like it?"

We'd decided to use a sixth-grader for the made-up party. That way there'd be even less of a chance that Karla would realize the information was faked. If the fifth-graders don't talk to Karla, the sixth-graders don't even know she's *alive*.

"What time does the party start?" Patti asked. "I've forgotten."

I glanced at Mr. Stamos out of the corner of my eye. He was taking it all in, all right. So was his wife behind the cash register. "At three o'clock," I replied, talking just a little louder than usual. "At the Health Club pool."

"I'll buy this card," Kate said, heading for the register.

"I think they took the bait!" Stephanie said under her breath as the four of us strolled out the door.

"We'll know for sure at three this afternoon," Kate said.

Stephanie, Patti, Kate, and I arrived at the Health Club about fifteen minutes early. We changed into our bathing suits and walked through the dressing room to the pool.. It's covered by one of those big, transparent bubbles, so even when it's freezing cold outdoors, it's warm as summer inside. We sat down on some deck chairs and waited for Karla to show up.

We didn't have to wait long. At three on the dot Karla walked in. She was wearing old gray sweats and carrying her brown notebook. She peered at the pool, which was almost empty except for Mark Freedman's little sister, Jessica, and a couple of other first-graders and their moms. Then her gaze fell on us, and she took one step back.

"Stephanie!" Karla said, trying to sound casual. "And Lauren and Kate and Patti. Are you here for Heather Fordman's party?"

"Heather's not having a party, Karla," Stephanie said evenly.

Karla moved closer, frowning. "Not having a party! But I heard. . . ." She stopped herself.

"From your aunt and uncle at the Party Store?!" Kate said sternly. "Well, it isn't true. We made the whole thing up."

Karla's eyes widened. "I . . . I . . . ," she stammered.

"Karla, that was a great way to get party news,"

Stephanie said. "But it was kind of sneaky not to tell me about it, wasn't it? We're co-reporters, remember?"

Karla started talking really fast. "I know I'm not very popular at school. That's why I volunteered for 'Social Notes.' I thought kids might start inviting me to parties." She took a deep breath. "If they didn't, I figured my aunt and uncle could let me know when somebody was having one, and I'd go anyway. Then you volunteered, Stephanie. Everybody likes you. The Party Store was the only advantage I had." Karla blushed bright red. "I know how you feel about me, Stephanie — I saw your letter in 'Q&A.' "

"At least somebody knew who I was talking about," Stephanie muttered. She eyed Karla for a minute. Then she said in a louder voice, "I guess I was competing a little, too, Karla. Some of the things I said in that letter were because I was afraid you were a better writer than I was. Look — I think 'X' was right," she gave Kate a friendly poke in the ribs. "We're stuck with each other for the next few weeks. And I think maybe we can learn something from each other . . . but we have to share information from now on. Right?"

"Right," said Karla, looking incredibly relieved.

"Shake?" said Stephanie, standing up and holding out her hand.

"Shake," said Karla, shaking hands with the beginnings of a smile on her face.

"Fine — why don't we all go swimming?" Stephanie suggested.

"Oh — I didn't bring a suit," Karla said.

"The club furnishes tank suits," Stephanie said helpfully.

"I'll show you, Karla," Patti offered, leading her toward the dressing room.

Kate raised an eyebrow. "Still getting to know the competition?" she said as Stephanie stepped onto the diving board.

"Nope," Stephanie said. "I felt kind of sorry for Karla when she said all that stuff. After all, I always have you guys and Karla doesn't have anybody." She dove into the pool with hardly a splash, popped up, and stuck out her tongue at us. "Come on in — the water's great!"

Sleepover Friends forever!

#16 Kate's Crush

Keith Foley had walked into the dining room. He was wearing a dark-green sweatshirt, brown pants, and a camouflage cap. He was carrying a funny little hammer that was pointed on one end and flat on the other.

As soon as he spotted us watching him he froze in his tracks. Stephanie smiled brightly and waved. With a scowl on his face, Keith turned around and ran out of the room.

"Wasn't that Keith?" Kate asked as she sat down at the table again.

Stephanie nodded. Then she looked at me and giggled.

"Come on, Stephanie. Eat your breakfast and leave Keith Foley alone," Kate said sternly.

"I wish I could figure out what's going on with him," Patti said, sliding into her chair. "He's a real mystery man. . . ."

WIN FIVE NIGHTSHIRTS FOR YOUR NEXT SLEEPOVER!

SLEEPOVER FRIENDS

Enter the SLEEPOVER FRIENDS Super Summer Giveaway

200 Winners!

"What's your favorite thing to do at a sleepover party?"

Make your next sleepover the best ever with FIVE fabulous, oversized Sleepover Friends nightshirts for you and four friends. It's easy to win! Just tell us what's *your* favorite thing to do at a sleepover party—like telling spooky ghost stories, or doing super makeovers! Then all you have to do to enter the Sleepover Friends Super Summer Giveaway is complete the coupon below and return by November 30, 1989.

Rules: Entries must be postmarked by November 30, 1989. Winners will be picked at random from all eligible entries received. No purchase necessary. Valid only in the U.S.A. Employees of Scholastic Inc., affiliates, subsidiaries, and their families are not eligible. Void where prohibited. Winners will be notified by mail.

Fill in the coupon below or write the information on a 3″ x 5″ piece of paper and mail to: SLEEPOVER FRIENDS SUPER SUMMER GIVEAWAY, Scholastic Inc., P.O. Box 665, Cooper Station, New York, NY 10276.

Sleepover Friends Super Summer Giveaway

What's your favorite thing to do at a sleepover party?

Check one:
☐ Eating ☐ Cooking ☐ Telling Ghost Stories
☐ Makeovers ☐ Truth or Dare ☐ Other _____

Name _____ Age _____

Street _____

City, State, Zip _____

Where did you buy this *Sleepover Friends* book?
☐ Bookstore ☐ Drug Store ☐ Supermarket ☐ Other _____
☐ Book Fair ☐ Book Club ☐ Discount Store

SLE289

Pack your bags for fun and adventure with

SLEEPOVER FRIENDS™

by Susan Saunders

Join Kate, Lauren, Stephanie and Patti at their great sleepover parties every weekend. Truth or Dare, scary movies, late-night boy talk—it's all part of **Sleepover Friends!**

America's Favorite Series

THE BABY-SITTERS CLUB®

by Ann M. Martin

Collect Them All!

The seven girls at Stoneybrook Middle School get into all kinds of adventures...with school, boys, and, of course, baby-sitting!

Available wherever you buy books...or use the coupon below.

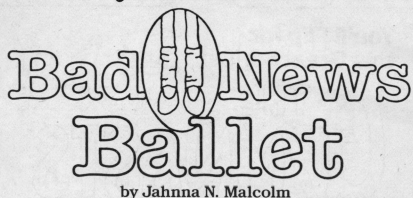